THIS BOOK BELONGS TO:

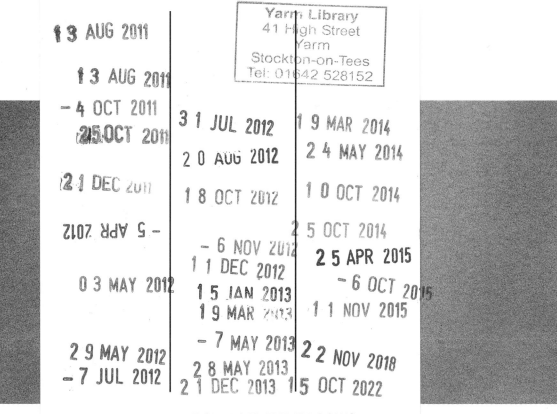
D0256478

This paperback edition published in 2011 by Andersen Press Ltd.

First published in Great Britain in 1990 by Andersen Press Ltd.,

20 Vauxhall Bridge Road, London SW1V 2SA.

Published in Australia by Random House Australia Pty.,

Level 3, 100 Pacific Highway, North Sydney, NSW 2060.

Text and Illustration copyright © Michael Foreman, 1990

The rights of Michael Foreman to be identified as the author and illustrator

of this work have been asserted by him in accordance with the

Copyright, Designs and Patents Act, 1988.

All rights reserved. Colour separated in Switzerland by Photolitho AG, Zürich.

Printed and bound in Singapore by Tien Wah Press.

Michael Foreman has used watercolour in this book.

10   9   8   7   6   5   4   3   2   1

British Library Cataloguing in Publication Data available.

ISBN 978 1 84939 304 1

This book has been printed on acid-free paper

MICHAEL FOREMAN

ONE WORLD

ANDERSEN PRESS

One sky
One sun
One moon
One world

A little girl stood still at the edge of the world and looked up at the sun.
She watched it go down at the end of the day.

That night, she watched the moon rise and the stars come out.

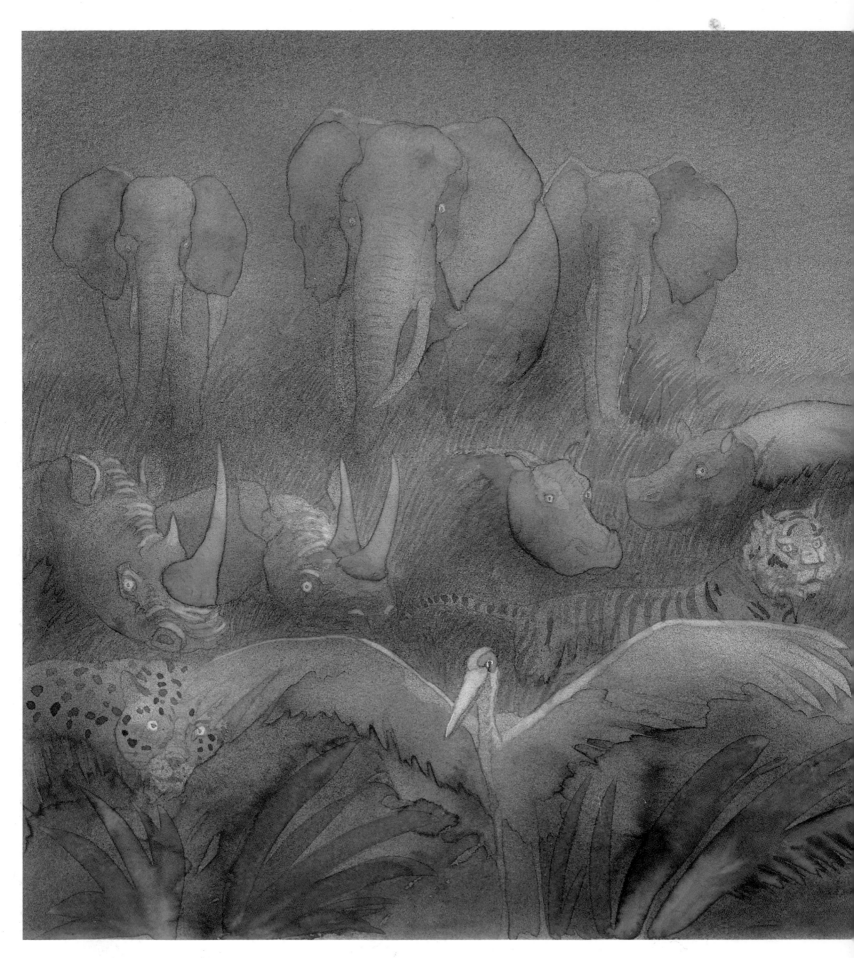

And as she watched, she thought of all the creatures who lived under the sky,

the animals who shared the warmth of the sun and bathed in the soft, silver light of the moon.

The next day the little girl and her brother stood at the edge of a pool by the sea.
They looked into the clear water.

The rocks in the pool stood like mountains, their peaks white with old barnacles.

Each time a wave washed through a gap in the rocks, dark forests of weeds waved as though they were trees in the wind. Tiny fish darted into the shadows past sea anemones like flowers in a secret garden.

"Look at that tin can," cried the boy. "It's a sunken ship full of buried treasure." And as they watched they saw starfish move slowly amongst a galaxy of shells and pebbles round as moons. On the surface of the pool, two feathers bobbed in a blob of oil.

The girl dipped her bucket into the pool and half filled it with water. She dropped a little sand into the bucket and watched it drift down to the bottom.

Her brother found stones covered in seaweed and put them in the bucket. Together the children watched the leaves swaying in the water. Then they added other kinds of seaweed and coloured stones and shells. They admired their tiny new world. But it still needed something. It needed more life.

So the boy chased a shrimp with his net.

He imagined the shrimp was a whale.

In a short time he caught two shrimps and three small fishes. He dropped them carefully into the bucket and watched them swim around.

The two children had made their own world. It was a new world with its own
forests, its own life.

Together, they held their world in their hands.

All the long afternoon, they tended their tiny world. They added more seaweed, shells and three more fish, but the more they added to their world, the more they took from the real world. The only things now floating in the pool were the feathers and the blob of oil.

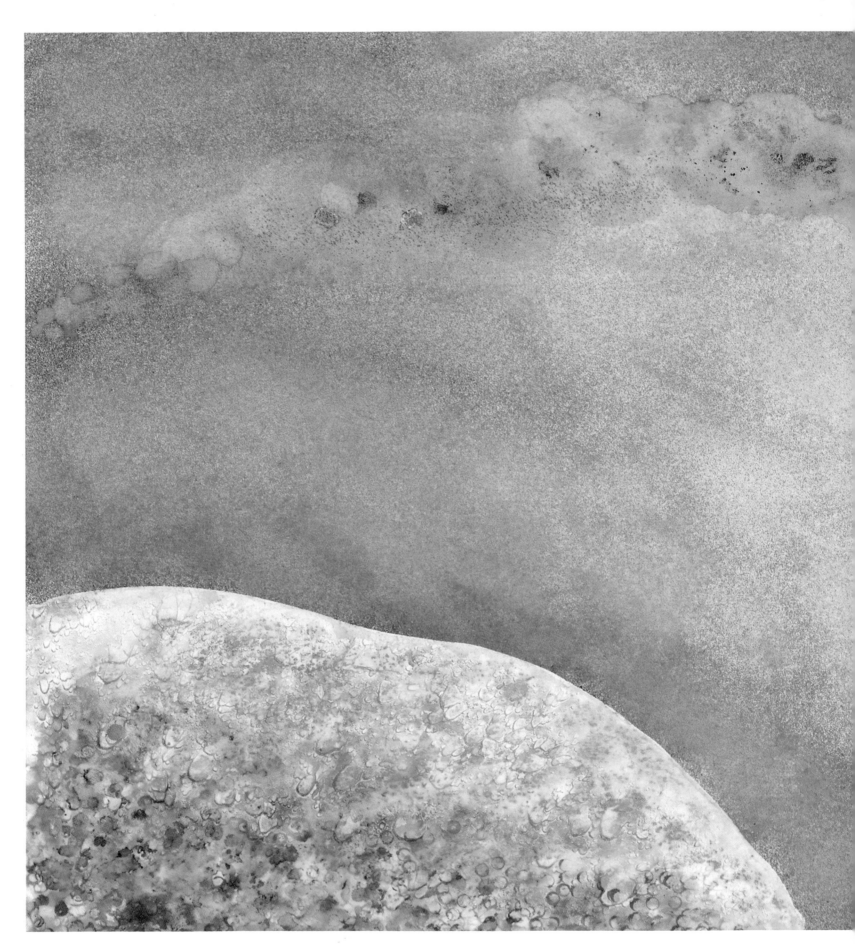

The oil had now spread across the surface and formed a rainbow over the upturned sky of the pool. But as it spread the pool began to turn cloudy and the

constellations of shells and starfish disappeared, just as the moon and stars are hidden when the forests of the world are burned.

The pool which had reminded the children of the beauty of the world, now showed how easily it could be spoiled.

It reminded them of the larger world they knew, where forests were disappearing in the clouds of smoke and people in towns were poisoning the land and the seas. A world where creatures even in far off snows and the deepest oceans were not safe.

Their little pools seemed so small, and the world so big. Just a drop in the ocean, really.
"What can we do?" cried the boy.
"You could help me," said the girl, and together they removed the tin can and dropped

one feather and the blob into it. They used the other feather to skim off the oily rainbow. Carefully, they returned all the things from the bucket to the larger world of the pool. Soon the tide would return and join the pool to the wide world of the ocean.

The children left the beach as the day cooled and the sun sank into the sea. Their bucket held only the tin, the oil and the feathers. They wondered what the evening tide would bring.

In the morning they would check all the pools. "We can ask the other children to help," said the girl.

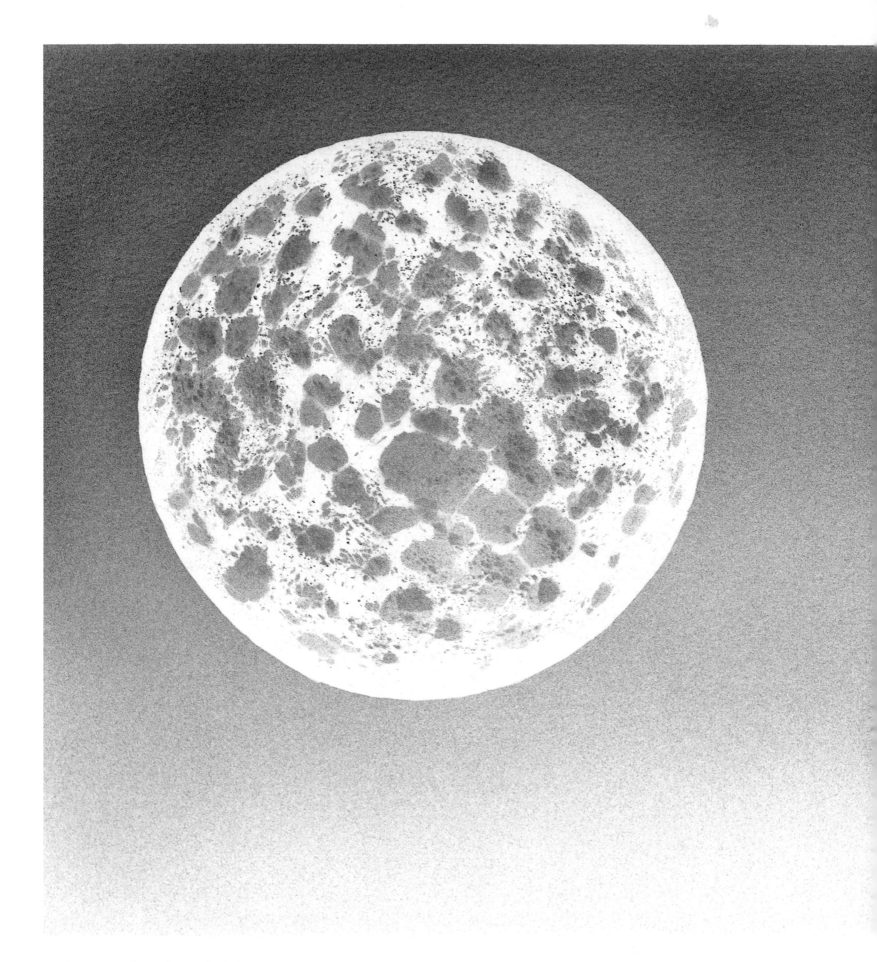

That night the children watched the moon and the stars. They thought about all the other children who lived under the sky, who needed the warmth of the sun

and the soft, silver light of the moon.

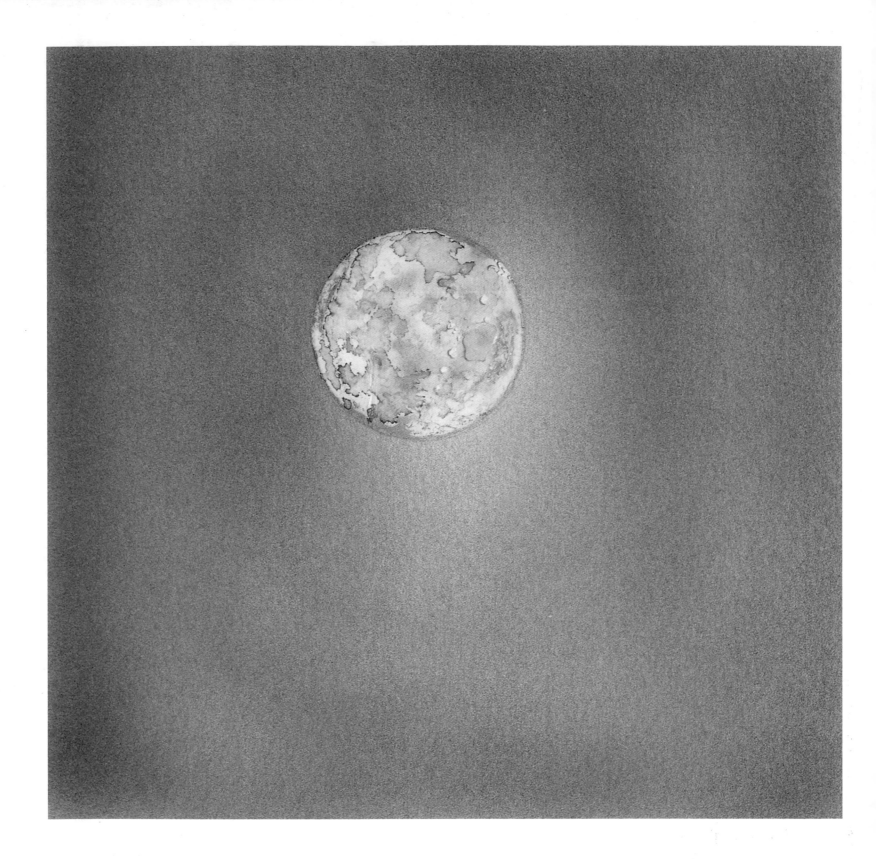

They all lived on one world.
And that world too, they held in their hands.